The Shrine

To: Myrna, Dad, Jim and Kirby

The Shrine

By Carl Birk

Cooper Townes' passion was the love of baseball.
He dreamed of the "Hall of Fame", his plaque upon the wall.
Cooper's athletic skills seemed to be off by a bit.
Many felt that baseball and Cooper just didn't fit.

In the summer you'd find him on the baseball field.
Playing his heart out with vigor and zeal.
He would imitate his heroes and vision himself a star.
His teammates wished he'd go home early in his family's car.

He believed he was Bob Feller when he took to the mound.
Till the ball shot past him, his butt upon the ground.
Cooper threw that ball again with all of his might.
And watched as the ball sailed well out of sight.

Cooper tried to be Ted Williams, giving the ball a mighty blast.
He could never figure out why he always batted last.
He thought he was speedy, like the fleet footed Lou Brock.
When Cooper stole second, he ran like a rock.

Cooper tried the outfield like fearless Reggie Jackson.
When the ball was hit in the air, he would take action.
Cooper chased down each fly, he thought it was fun.
Until he ran into his teammate, the ball lost in the sun.

The coach put him at shortstop like the great Honus Wagner.
Honus was agile and talented, but Cooper was neither.
The ball was hit at him and he had an easy peg.
That was until that sphere shot right between his legs.

With another loss looming, his team in great despair.
The coach was now fuming and pulling out his hair.
He shouted out loud, "Townes take behind the plate."
"Not a ball gets by you son or the dugout is your fate."

Cooper strapped on the equipment, which fit like a glove.
He stepped towards home plate for the sport that he loved.
No one on the team ever wanted the catcher position.
This was Cooper's final baseball audition.

Townes bent down slowly, into a comfortable squat.
In his stomach there seemed to grow a large knot.
The batter took a swing for a mighty big hit.
To Cooper's surprise the ball popped into his mitt.

Next thing he remembered someone stealing second base.
Cooper threw the ball swiftly, the runner was erased.
He protected that plate and the space that he roamed.
Rarely did an opponent ever touch home.

The coach now took interest and taught Cooper the ropes.
Townes now believed once again in his Hall of Fame hopes.
He reduced his errors by working really hard.
Someday he envisioned being on a baseball card.

Townes went to the batting cage and learned how to hit.
He became a vacuum cleaner stopping all with his mitt.
Cooper's arm was like lightning, some say the very best.
Scouts started to notice him from the east to the west.

The reporters started comparing him to Berra and to Bench.
The backstop he guarded his feet were entrenched.
Any runner who stormed home, faced a true collision.
Sprawled on the ground tagged out, oh a bad decision.

Cooper eventually played high school and in the minors.
Everywhere he played he became a headliner.
He never did lose his passion for the game.
Cooper accepted all honors as well as some blame.

Cooper Townes ended up doing nothing wrong.
His fans erected statues and praised him in song.
He played in the majors for a very long time.
The Hall of Fame awaits him as part of the shrine.

The End